A Snowy Surprise

~ Book Three ~

New York

Illustrated by the Disney Storybook Artists
Designed by Deborah Boone

Printed in China

First Edition
3 5 7 9 10 8 6 4 2

ISBN 978-1-4231-2593-8
T425-2382-5-11124

For more Disney Press fun,
visit www.disneybooks.com

The fast-flying fairy Vidia loved to make fun of the other fairies. She called the garden fairies "petal-heads" and caterpillar herders "slowpokes." Vidia thought no other talent was as good as hers.

One day, after Vidia made a water fairy cry, Tink said angrily, "Vidia, someday you'll learn appreciate another talent."

Vidia just laughed. "Darling, that will happen when it snows in Pixie Hollow." Of course, she knew it never would, for it was always spring or summer in Pixie Hollow, where the fairies lived.

Until one day . . .

Lily was the first to notice it. As usual, she had risen early to go out and enjoy her garden. She was just settling down to watch the grass grow when a dark cloud crossed the sun.

"Looks like rain," Lily said.

But then a shiver passed through her wings. "Hmm?" she said, rubbing her bare arms. "Why is it so cold?"

"Look, Lily!" exclaimed Rosetta, flying into Lily's garden. She held out her hand to show Lily a lacy white crystal. For a second, the crystal glistened in the morning light. Then, in a blink, it melted into a puddle in Rosetta's palm.

Lily held out her hand and caught one, too.

"What in Never Land is going on?" asked Rosetta.

Before long, a thin layer of white had covered the ground, and most of Pixie Hollow had come out to behold the sight.

As more and more of the lacy white flakes fell, the fairies reached out to try to catch them. A few brave souls even took a taste.

"*Hmph*. Rather bland," said Dulcie, a baking-talent fairy, who'd been hoping the crystals would taste as delicious and sugary as they looked. "I wonder what they could be?" she wondered.

"Don't you know?" said Prilla. "It's snow!"

"Snow?" said the fairies. "But it never snows in Never Land." They shivered as the white flakes continued to fall.

"What do we do now?" a sparrow man wondered.

"We play in it, of course!" said Prilla. She scooped up a handful of snow. With a twinkle in her eye, she tossed it at her friend Tinker Bell. It landed with a soft splat on Tink's green dress.

Tink laughed. "Watch out, Prilla! Now it's my turn!" Soon all the fairies had joined in the snowball fight.

But the fairies found that the snow was too cold to play in for long. So the sewing-talent fairies set to work making hats and scarves from mouse wool, while the cobbler-talent fairies fashioned cozy boots out of moss. The fairies all agreed that their new outfits were quite fetching, and they hurried outside to put them to use.

"Moon and stars!" exclaimed the light-talent fairy Fira. "Just look at the Home Tree!"

The fairies' great tree seemed to sparkle like a palace made of jewels! Every broad green leaf wore a veil of shimmering frost, while icicles dripped from the branches like diamonds.

As she took in the sight, Fira's glow flashed bright silver in appreciation.

By now the snow was wing-deep, and the art-talent fairies had discovered another use for the white flakes.

"You can sculpt with it!" shouted Bess as she a built a perfect snow-fairy, complete with wings made from sheets of frosted spider web.

"This one will be you!" she called to Tinker Bell.

At Havendish Steam, the fairies found that the usually bubbling ribbon of water was as smooth as glass.

"Look," said the water fairy Rani. She tapped her toe on the ice. "It's hard . . . and slippery too!" Bravely, she stepped out onto the surface of the frozen stream and glided across it.

"Come on!" she called to the others. "This is almost as fun as flying!"

Meanwhile, in the meadow, the fast-flying talents were busy whipping down the slopes on sleds made of magnolia leaves. Even Vidia joined in, for she could never resist a race.

"You can't catch me, darlings! Don't even try! What fun!" she cried as she zipped ahead.

By mid-afternoon, every fairy in Pixie Hollow was enjoying the snow. But there was still one thing they hadn't figured out.

"I wonder where the snow is coming from," said Tinker Bell as she slid down a snowy slope with Terence.

Terence shrugged. "Maybe we'll never know."

"Vidia!" Rani said as the fast-flying fairy slid to a stop. "Could it be that you finally appreciate another fairy's talent?"

"Whatever do you mean?" asked Vidia.

Rani pointed to the sky, where a group of water fairies were turning falling raindrops into snowflakes. "You said that you'd appreciate another fairy's talent when it snowed in Pixie Hollow," Rani reminded Vidia. "You can thank the water fairies for your fun!"

"You know, Rani," Tink said a little bit later. "I think Vidia *does* appreciate your talent."

Rani smiled. "Even though she'll never admit it."